# David and the
# Kittens

## Robert Westall

*Illustrated by*
## William Geldart

Hodder
Children's
Books

A division of Hodder Headline Limited

'Furble's getting fat,' said David. 'Furble's having kittens,' said Gran. 'Shall we have to have the vet?' asked David, alarmed. 'Lord love you, no. She'll know what to do. She's a farm-cat born and bred. And a grand ratter. They say good ratters make good mothers.'

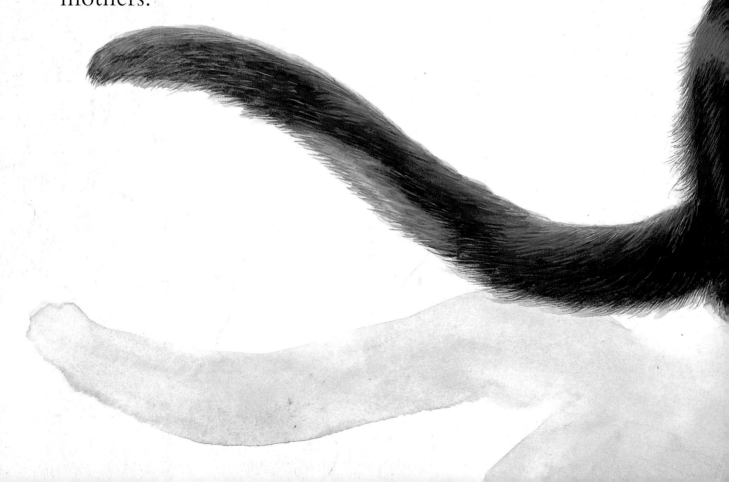

Furble grew fatter.

'She's shaped like a pear,' said David.

'She's like a pod,' said Gran. 'A pod full of peas.
Feel. Gently. You can feel all the little heads.'

David counted four.

As the days passed, Furble gave up ratting.
She just sat and washed and washed her white
belly-fur. Bare pink patches began appearing.
'She's wearing her fur away licking,' said David.
'That's so the kittens will know where to feed,'
said Gran. 'Look, you can see her nipples clear.'

When Furble had grown so fat she
couldn't grow any fatter, Gran got
the usual place ready – the bottom
drawer of the kitchen cupboard.
Furble sat in the shadowed part
of the drawer, looking broody.
She began to pant,
and then tried to climb
out of the drawer
onto Gran's knee.

'They'll have them on
your knee, if you let
them,' said Gran.
She put Furble back
firmly, sat on the floor
and stroked the cat.
'They like their
humans near.'

Then suddenly Furble shuddered and kicked out
her back legs and there was a transparent sausage
on the end of a string. With a kitten trapped inside.
'What do we do?' yelled David.
'Watch,' said Gran.
Furble doubled round like a hoop.
Her white teeth flashed on
the struggling sausage.
'She's killing it. She's
eating it,' shouted
David. 'Help.'

But the next second the sausage was empty, and a tiny wet mouse-like thing was feebly struggling on the wet paper, towards the bulk of its mother. And Furble's huge tongue was licking it on and helping it. David had never seen anything so weak and helpless.

'Four,' said Gran. 'I thought there were four.
       Two little ginger toms, a black tom,
              and a little white female, I reckon.'

The kittens grew and grew further. Slowly their ears, folded to their skulls, opened like little petals. Behind their slits, the blind eyes bulged and moved. They lay on the old blanket in the drawer. Their tails, from being thin and rat-like, grew into fat little triangles.

'Why do they never stop wriggling?'

'To get into the middle where it's warmest.'

David had invented a game. As soon as Furble and Gran left the kitchen, he picked up the kittens from their tight wriggling heap, and put one in each corner of the drawer. Immediately, their squeaking started. And then, still blind, by rolling, falling, crawling, paddling along their fat little bodies, they found each other again, and the squeaking stopped, and the wriggling of the heap started again.

'Don't pick them up too much, or they'll smell of you, not Furble,' said Gran. 'Then she might reject them. She might even kill them.'

David felt guilty.

On the tenth day, Gran said: 'Watch their eyes. They should open today. Once their ears are up, their eyelids split.'

And by the evening, some kittens had one-and-a-half eyes open, and others no more than a glinting slit. But the oddest thing was, once the kittens' eyes were open, they refused to stay in their tight squirming ball, and began endless meandering crawls round the drawer. Furble kept picking them up by the scruff of the neck, and putting them back in the heap. 'Now her troubles are starting,' said Gran.

It was the black kitten who got out of the drawer first. 'They'll all be out tomorrow,' said Gran. 'We won't be able to move for kittens.'

Now the kittens were moving everywhere, far better at moving than in knowing where they were going. Furble kept picking them up, and they kept escaping again. She was frantic.

'I'll put them in the old tea chest to give her a bit of peace.'

David eyed the towering sides of the tea chest. 'They'll never get out of that.'

'I'll give them two days.

Two days of peace for her.

Two days of peace for us.'

Two days it was.

'Now's the time to find them homes,' said Gran.

'But they're far too young to leave her.'

'People who want kittens like to be in at the beginning.
They like to come every week and see how their kitten's
getting on. Here you are – magazines. We're looking for
pictures of kittens. Coloured pictures.'

'Five postcards,' said Gran. 'One each for the post office, the off-licence, the vet's, the corner-shop and the pet-shop in town.'

Then she wrote on each card:

VERY GOOD HOMES WANTED FOR ADORABLE KITTENS.

ROMULUS AND REMUS, twin ginger toms
LUCKY, a lucky black tom.
SNOWDROP, a pretty white female.

'All kittens are adorable,' she said. 'People just need reminding.'

'Why'd you give them names? People will want to give them their own names.'

'I know they will,' said Gran. 'But it all helps make the postcard more interesting. Now, run down to the shops with the postcards. Two weeks in each shop. That should do it.'

And it did.

The phone rang two nights later.

The family came round. Gran gave
them coffee; the kittens wavered
and wobbled round their feet.
'I'd like the little white one,' said
the little girl.

'I've always wanted a lucky
black tom,' her mum said.
'I've always fancied ginger
toms,' said the father.

'I think you're very wise,' said Gran. 'They'll be good company for each other. They'll have you in fits with their antics.' She gave the father her most winning smile.

After that there wasn't much argument. The family departed asking if they could come back in a week, to see how their kittens were getting on.

'I like kittens to go in pairs,' said Gran. 'It's terrible what happens to single kittens. One day they've got their mum and all their brothers and sisters, and the next they are alone among strangers. That's when you've got to love them and cuddle them non-stop or …'

'Or what?'

'Or else they turn
into very dull cats, who
just don't like anybody.
I've seen too many cats
like that.'

A couple came at the weekend. And chose the lucky black
tom. But they didn't want the little white female and nor,
it seemed, did anybody else.

David began to worry. What if they couldn't find a home?

'Oh, well,' said Gran. 'Maybe we'll keep her for ourselves.
Trouble is, that way, I could end up one of those ladies with
twenty cats.'

But it got forgotten
in the fun of
the riotous time.

What Gran called 'thunder of hooves time':
kittens chasing each other everywhere, leaping on
each other, crashing each other down, lying in ambush,
waggling their tiny bottoms, pouncing.

Kittens could do so many things cats couldn't. Running sideways like crabs, running backwards, leaping two feet in the air from a standing four-footed start. Climbing Gran's curtains right to the top and then yowling because they couldn't get down again. Gran had to rescue them twenty times a day.

'They purr like little bees. They spit like little fireworks.'
'Yes, they're almost ready to go. If only for Furble's sake. They've worn her out, poor love.'

They taught them to drink milk,
upending them and
plunging their noses
into the saucer.

The kittens, released, would sneeze milk all over.
then lick their noses with their tiny tongues.

Later David helped rub cat food on their faces. They soon got the idea of that, too.

Kittens got trodden on, sat on by the vicar when he called. You could not move for kittens. Furble began to attack the kittens. Finally, they made a fort under Gran's chair, and kept driving off their mother with fierce blows. But when she tried to rest, they leapt fiercely and bit her tail.
'Time to go,' said Gran.

David sat in the silent kitchen.

Snowdrop lay in a chair, asleep. She had spent a lot of the morning wandering around, looking for the others and mewing sadly. She looked very small and grown-up and lonely as she lay asleep.

David picked her up and put her on his knee and stroked her gently with one finger. It would never do to have Snowdrop turn into a dull, boring cat. Like a tiny bee, Snowdrop began to purr.

It would be all right:
just a lot of loving
to do.

British Library Cataloguing in Publication Data
A catalogue record of this book is available from the British Library.

ISBN 0 340 74379 4  (HB)
ISBN 0 340 74380 8 (PB)

First published as 'David and the Kittens' in *Cat's Whispers and Tales,* Macmillan 1996.

Published in 2003
by Hodder Children's Books,
a division of Hodder Headline Limited,
338 Euston Road, London NW1 3BH

10 9 8 7 6 5 4 3 2 1

Printed in Hong Kong